TWENTY–NINE

by

Aaron Doolittle

FICTION

Truth is no better than art.

To the unfortunate truth, equal parts beautiful and hideous; that which will never be more important than art.

And for my moms.

I, a gentle ticking turned into a bang, a drip of water turned into a stream.

It begins on a Monday at a point where the outside observer has to assume this is the moment where the narrative begins. Even though everything prior to this moment is essential, these details are carefully guarded intentionally kept from the observer in order to indicate that the journey is going to demand commitment.

At two in the morning he sits in the bathtub of some cheap hotel while water hits him in the face because the shower is on. He feels tired and isn't sure he can move. The thought of getting to his feet is inhibiting, moving means action, forward momentum is preemptive, for better or worse.

He lies in the tub while he looks up at a girl as she showers. She turns away from him, her neck tilts down and she washes between her legs and it makes him think: delicate, decent, polite. This might be the first moment in a long time when he sees a feminine gesture and thinks: grace, poise, allure.

Does it seem misogynistic? Is sexist the same thing? If a race is defined by certain upbringings that carry over from generation to generation, is the observed reoccurring traits based on upbringing still racism?

What's important is that while he lays there, a woman, naked, washing herself, smiling at him, talking about whatever might have happened last night has turned away from him to wash herself, because some girls close their eyes so tightly when they make love to the person they desire, some women are inhibited to the point of hiding even without a stitch of clothing on their lovely body, they hide behind their hair, they squeeze their eyes shut, they hide their face behind his, sucking on his neck.

She stands under the shower rinsing her hair. There are girls who do all that; but then there are others. Consider the girls who use showmanship to mask insecurity—the hollow fucking, is no worse, no better.

It begins here with reason. People infer where a story is headed to understand and create a familiarity. There are rules to maintain when asking the commitment of an outside viewer because all relationships are based on trust. There are narratives that cater to the outside observer compromising integrity and identity at whatever cost in order to appeal to a mass-market, then there are narratives in which everything is so carefully engrained in the story that beginners cannot fully compute the information and understand its nature until the story is finished.

So imagine there are two types of women, one that hides themselves during sex or those that make a spectacle of themselves during the act. A million little variables separate each woman from the next, maybe they are expressive but compassionate, maybe they are self-conscious but desire dirty sexy domination.

Every case unto itself, and only in the event that the narrative treats its characters the same does it maintain an appropriate basis in reality.

Having established both ends of the spectrum, it begins here for a reason.

There in the shower when she turns away from him to wash her cunt, he grabs a support bar screwed into the tiled wall and pulls himself to his feet, he soaps up his hands and begins to wash her back.

His fingertips felt strange, distant as if unattached. Her skin was soft and smooth, separated by time; a woman in her thirties felt different than a woman in her twenties. Like a helix the two at different points in their lives have skin that feels different, not bad. Maybe the younger woman's body generates a greater sexual energy while the flesh belonging to the older woman knows itself and can inspire a beauty and pleasure not yet accessible to the girl with the tits as firm as ripe fruit.

They were somewhere in a lesser part of town.

She had a small apartment filled with thrift store furniture that she loved and each piece unto its own smacked of charm and kitsch. But nothing really belonged. No two pieces shared a common era or design, somehow each stick of furniture lived separate lives until this apartment. Simply put, an illogical series of random events where by people abandoned once loved possessions and set them at the curb or gave them to goodwill just in time for their most current owner the Diane, now in her forties, would drive by and see the armchair sitting out on garbage-day, or to find the endearingly hideous lamp while perusing the aisles at Am-vets. It was those fated moments that brought the apartment's furniture together.

He liked being there. He didn't care much for interior design; a place was a place was a place, but with Diane he liked lying there afterwards. There was a stillness with Diane as if the before and the during and the after were no less than any single moment. And not that 'her' implies a certain sentimental 'her' as if there were none other, but 'her' in this context, being Diane, the girl he liked to lay with after, exuded a certain energy that calmed his constant worry. She was no more *her* than the one before or the next that follows.

She laid face down on the bed, awake but dreaming of sleep while he ran his fingers up and down the small of her back. The bed was dressed in white sheets while her long blonde hair sprawled out like a roman candle, the small of her back made up of lean, perfectly defined muscle, her body otherwise soft and feminine.

Outside, the bell of a nearby church chimed eight and despite the sound from an outside world coming into the little room in the bad part of town time stood still.

It is early on Wednesday. Charles gets to his feet, and seems confused by the morning sun coming through the front windows of a living room he doesn't recognize. He pulls on his jeans as a thin-limbed woman collects empty beer bottles in the next room and because she has her back to him he's not sure what her name is.

Perhaps if he could see her face he would recognize her. Nothing is familiar. Even his clothes, having worn them so many days in a row feel as if they belonged to someone else.

He checks for his wallet at the same time finds his keys. The thin-limbed woman carries a collection of empty beer bottles threaded between her fingers and goes into the kitchen.

Charles almost makes out her profile but his eyes are swollen and itchy.

The next day he finds himself looking out at the trees in Jolene's backyard. The trees sway in the breeze and the neighborhood's sounds remain mottled. A car passes but the sound is so far away it is an unperceivable buzz in the transient noise around them. There are birds in the trees and they speak to one another but they are so far off it is impossible to determine what type of birds they are or what they are saying to one another. It seems as if the world is under water while Charles sits on a kitchen chair on the back patio of Jolene's apartment.

Her feet make a slight shuffling sound as she sidesteps around him; the scissors make a thick slicing sound as she trims Charles thick dark hair. And Charles sits, peacefully; the moment is void of conversation, no pre-sexual intimacy or post-sexual energy. Charles is finally in the hands of an artist and his purpose is to remain still, focused on nothing, basking in serenity, the calm cool motion of her fingers through his hair pulling a few inches from the scalp, aligning the hairs with her first and second finger.

Slice.

Charles wonders what day it is as Jolene moves around to his left and evens out the hair on both sides. He had been here before. Jolene and Charles had the beginnings of a relationship, without it lasting long enough to call it what it was. Charles liked her, she liked him and they shared a momentum that seemed to hold potential. But once they got over that first hill, once the dating and sleepovers turned into a quiet-night-in and uneventful mornings sipping tea, it became evident to them, almost simultaneously that they were very different people programmed to desire a very different type of person, something that neither of them could fake or attempt to portray. It was a peaceable end, and they were good to each other, from the start of that end they became friends. Charles loved when Jolene cut his hair, and Jolene liked doing it even though cutting hair was her nine-to-five. When he came around for a haircut in the afternoon they sat out on the porch watching the trees and listening to the sounds that seemed miles off, if it was too dark out they sat in the kitchen listening to old records. Charles never cared much what his hair looked like; just the same Jolene did a pretty good job.

*

TWENTY-NINE

His coworker's fat little fingers pick up another paperclip. Charles knows his coworker has a name but if asked about him, it would take a full moment after hearing the name that Charles would be able to bring to mind the fat man's face.

What no one else knows is that Charles refers to his coworker as The Twat, (pronounced with a short A as if said with a British accent). No one knows this because Charles doesn't discuss his job with anyone but himself, his inner monologue is unending, and his opinion of everything around him (at least when he's sober) is generally hostile.

The fat man in the half cubicle across the industrial blue carpet threads the paperclip through another paperclip making a useless chain one bit longer.

Charles stares at his computer screen while The Twat speaks about something, and though Charles gives no indication he is listening, no eye contact, no sound of 'mhmm,' The Twat continues his commentary and Charles feels this conversation could be a form of rape.

Conver-rape, or Conversational Rape: noun, when someone forces conversation on a person, or into a conversation without consent of the listener.

Ex: My mom's new boyfriend won't shut up about his radio controlled model airplanes, he must have conver-raped me for over twenty minutes.

Ex: My boss is really pushy, he never listens and talks about nothing; he's a real conver-rapist.

The Twat continues linking paperclips to the paperclip chain, the little yellow box that holds the paperclips, which he has taken from the office supply room is still nearly full.

"You can't let your kids move back home. There's no security in the real world, why should parents fake that..."

Charles continues staring at his computer monitor and the sound of it all goes in and out, as if an ocean wave brings the room tone to full volume and as the wave rolls back there is suddenly nothing, no sound, just Charles hearing nothing, looking at nothing, not sure what is real.

TWENTY-NINE

"...But then again when my parents were young they lived at home till it was time to get married, you know sometimes that could last into their..."

Charles is so hung-over that his mouth won't open unless he takes a sip of water.

"...Oh! It's five o'clock," says The Twat.

The fat man grabs his brief case and collects paperwork to take home with him. He has to lean forward before he stands; once he's up he adjusts his belt and puts a hand against Charles cubicle. He smiles like they are friends. Now that The Twat has come close enough that he verges on invading Charles personal space, Charles looks away from his computer up at the fat man and they look at each other both silent for several seconds.

The Twat says, "So, Chuck what are you going to do with your weekend?"

"Recover," Charles says without blinking.

"Hah, to have my twenties back."

Charles' eyes flutter, "I'm going to be thirty next month."

"Then you haven't got much time left, have you?"

The Twat begins to leave and Charles feeling defensive says each word with conviction, "I will never, have anything, even remotely in common with you or your life."

A moment passes; suppressing anger for a moment The Twat finds clarity, though still hurt, he says honestly,

"You're human aren't you?"

Charles just stares at the fat coworker, without saying a word to either confirm or deny the question.

*

Any two men, could be anyone really, as long as they are wearing suits that fit them, not that they are fitted because fitted suits imply upper class, good physic or high fashion; these men fit in suits. They belong in them. Other than button up shirts they own only Polos and khakis. They look strange in shorts, the only T-shirts they own are from Dave Matthews' concerts they went to back in college.

They are drinking beer, but they are not really drinking it. They are tasting it. It's happy hour and assuming they were drinking it the way a man opens his mouth and swallows his beer they might end up mildly inebriated, tipsy after a brew and a half, because they are not really drinking it, they are tasting it. Going home after work to have dinner with the wife can only be avoided for forty minutes at most, just a quick drink, not too many, otherwise she'll be disappointed that she has to sit and eat dinner with half a vacant lot for a husband, a lightweight half twisted on a beer and a half because of a lack of strength and an abused will, his tolerance whittled to nothing, and in this the fleeting glimpse of an alcohol buzz becomes momentous, nostalgic, because that life meant college (good times) and the fleeting glimpse of an alcohol buzz risks an upset in the home life (these times) at the risk of disappointing her; and not because she is mean or unruly but because 'she and he' are bound in the sacred trust of marriage they should never have separate lives, with this beer and a half comes a sense of rebellion, rebelling against the suit and the khakis, it is a vote against her insistence that he get rid of that worn out T-Shirt that says: Tripping Billies. And really it isn't about avoiding her, it's just about getting one fucking free minute away from work and away from home. There's a kindness in the moments where he is alone to himself, defined by nothing, sipping two-dollar bottle beers. And so he tastes his beer, and he's sorry he used the F-word, and he wonders quite often, if his fellow colleague who also looks most appropriate when wearing a suit, if he feels the same way about *his* marriage.

As Charles comes in the front door so does the light and for a second the true grit and rustic ambience of the bar is revealed. The bartender turns to the door,

"HANDSOME CHUCK!"

Charles shouts back, "Handsome Bastard!"

"The usual?"

And Charles quips, "In the company of the unusual."

The bartender is a mountain of a man, tall and broad shouldered, huge arms like nautical ropes. He was a local god in his hometown back east and he would commute to Toronto trying his hand at professional wrestling. He liked being the bad guy. He would come out into the venue and talk shit like a sick-minded villain. He challenged anyone he ran into to meet him in the ring, man, woman, small or large. While inside his true nature was warm and hospitable; he was a good old boy that men and women alike wanted to be around. He loved the adrenaline in the ring. A friend told him to move out to LA and work as a stuntman so he could put together some money while making his way.

His stage name was Tommy Hawk, his given name is Devin and he has worked as a bartender for the last twenty odd years.

Tommy Hawk pours a beer and a shot of whiskey as Charles hops onto a bar stool, the two men wearing suits watch this because it's the only thing that's happened inside the bar over the last twenty minutes.

Charles knows they are watching him, unsure why, it doesn't make much difference. Charles is used to being watched and that has made his skin grow thicker than most. Tommy brings Charles the shot and the beer, Tommy sets the two in front of Charles and they shake hands.

Neither of the two men in suits touch their drinks, they are unaware that they have been starring at the only other two in the bar, yet it happens fast enough that it doesn't seem queer (queer as in strange).

Charles drinks the shot and then throws his head back and floors the full glass of beer.

"Jesus-fucking-Christ."

Charles wipes his chin and turns to look at the man in the suit, the man only then realizes he cursed out loud and now the man is smiling all awkward and self-conscious.

Charles asks, "You've never seen a chaser before?"

Tommy takes the two empty glasses, turns, and with his back to the suits Tommy pours another round.

This time it's the second man in the suit,

"I've never understood chasers."

His colleague, "I've seen them, I understand them but, Jesus, an entire beer?"

The other man says, "I'm of the mind, if you drink, drink one or the other. If a shot's too strong drink something else. You understand me right? It's like, you know, be all in."

The two men in suits sip their beer and smack their lips and say 'ahh' while the bartender shakes his head and brings Charles a second round. Charles doesn't acknowledge Tommy but it's not like earlier in the day when Charles wouldn't look at his coworker The Twat. Charles and Tommy share a closeness that would be cheapened with a 'thank you.'

Charles and Tommy though at very different points in their lives are connected by time and space, they were of the same tribe in a previous life, in another time they used to hunt predatory felines and they would bring home their kill to feed their wives. And so Tommy can already tell that Charles wants to get into it with these two men in suits, but he won't out of respect because it's Tommy's bar and Charles could be called a lot of things, but the one thing he is always, is loyal.

"You ever been in love?" Charles asks the suits.

Holding up his left hand one of the men says, "I'm married."

Charles asks again, "You ever been in *love*?"

Frustrated the guy in the suit says, "Are you deaf?"

With a sideways smirk Charles says, "I've probably already heard more than you've said-- I ask you if you've been in love and you say you're married." Charles shakes his head here, just before he gets to it, "I don't mean your soul mate, I mean that one girl that was a total wild child, beyond reason and logic, the one girl that you fell for the minute you saw her. Not love that grows, love that kills. "

Charles holds up his shot glass and looks through the caramel colored spirit that glows amber as it passes in line with an overhead light. The drink glows vivid. He drinks the shot and holds up the empty glass,

"This is the girl that won't let you love her. And if you pursue her she'll eventually destroy you. There's only one way to keep going if you're willing to try. You're going to need a back-up."

Charles gestures at the beer, presenting it to make his point, then he drinks the beer in one shot.

*

The world is slightly smaller than it used to be. And it's harder to follow a person's meaning. For everything that gets said a million little meanings can be inferred. Or is it when a person is straight forward, is that the most misleading a person can be? When there is no subtext, only then will men and women stand a fighting chance of achieving a shared goal. That is the utopia in which the war of the sexes reaches a standstill.

Charles sits on the floor with his back against a recliner, his mind is racing in all directions and every time he comes to his original point it seems mystifying like a coincidence too eerie to just be: something that happens.

Keira sits on the floor as well, about four feet from Charles, and she's listening. She doesn't exactly understand his meaning, or even what he is saying because all of it seems vague or indirect, like he's not saying what he means, or that he is setting it up in some overly complicated way, she thinks she follows him but every little tangent or off topic thing he references seems to have some impossible connection. The illogical conversation makes her think of laying in the grass and looking up at clouds, she remembers staring up at the clouds and imagining they appear in shapes that resemble turtles or dinosaurs or naked gods and goddesses, and while she suddenly has such a vivid memory of looking up at the clouds she wonders if that is her own memory or an experience so engrained in the iconic American childhood that she has sold herself a false memory. Yet she must have, if she remembers lying in the grass looking up at the clouds, right? But every time she tries to visualize the memory it looks like a film or a cartoon, the sky is an unnatural blue and the grass too green to be real, she can't remember how old she would have been, and she can't remember who she would have been lying there with. Was the grass short and coarse or was she surrounded by tall, tall grass, and by that time she hasn't the faintest idea what Charles is saying.

"I think that people don't keep what's important in their sights. I think they go from day to day fighting through deadlines, and dinners they don't want to be at, and rehearsed answers are all we ever say, when really we need to just keep in mind what we're looking forward to. You have to know at any moment, what is the next thing you're looking forward to. Because if you don't--"

Kiera leans so far over, she lands on her side and she takes the pipe from Charles hand, still talking Charles hands her the lighter. She packs the little bit left with the bottom of her lighter and interrupting him she says, "You're different."

"No, I'm not," Charles says.

"I didn't say it was a bad thing," Kiera smokes the last of the pot, holds it in her lungs for a beat and then exhales. Charles is quiet now, self-conscious, not insecure, but self-conscious wondering how and if he has changed.

Kiera sets down the pipe on a coffee table, leans onto her hands and crawls towards Charles. The small of her back peaks out from the top of her jeans as she slowly creeps into his lap. She buries her head in his chest and leans her weight on her calves, with her hands she unbuttons Charles fly-- four buttons and her hand is in his jeans, she tries to pull him out and it is awkward as his body is ready and it won't give in any direction but one. She puts him in her mouth and goes down hard; ascending she gently drags her teeth against his skin.

Charles shuts his eyes and mediates almost unaffected. He listens to her, feels how deep inside her he can feel, and he wonders how he has changed. She goes down on him another minute, her passion heightens even though Charles hasn't touched her, he can tell. He is unsure if he has changed and it makes him self-conscious.

Sure of one thing, in order to prove that he hasn't changed, he is obligated to do this, now, well and full of passion. That's how he hasn't changed.

Pushing her off him he lays her on her back and pulls off her jeans, her cute underwear goes unnoticed, her clean smooth skin is freshly showered and shaven meaning this moment is not entirely spontaneous.

Charles climbs on top of her and kisses her lips so gently they are barely touching. A faint trace of saliva allows their lips to pass gently over each other's and before he even kisses her with his mouth she has her hands between his legs positioning him such that without resistance he is inside her.

The insides of his muscles still scratched with adrenaline, that old familiar sensation was still in full throws, his breath still shallow and labored lying on his back naked and sweating. Kiera gets up on one knee and pulls an afghan off a recliner, she wraps it around her midsection and as she walks out of the living room says, "Goodnight, Chuck."

Charles sits up still catching his breath and asks, "We going to bed?"

"Yep. You're on the couch," she says as she goes out of the room.

Charles sits up and looks at the living room, realizing for the first time that there is no couch, but a chair and a loveseat and the loveseat is less than four feet wide. He gets up, still naked his body damp and stinking of sex and so he attempts curling up on the love seat. His legs are bent and his neck crooked. He blinks a few times and considers if he is sober enough to drive, because he's pissed and uncomfortable and wants to leave; but if he left where could he go?

Charles wakes on the floor, somewhere, wherever his pants are his cell phone is vibrating. Charles pushes himself up off the floor in one fluid movement. Finding his pants he digs out his phone and looks at the caller ID. It must be morning because the sun is up.

*

The kitchen had been changed, redone, three times since he was a child. His father had redone most of the house over the past ten years, going from one room to the next changing one bedroom into a study, his father's original smaller study became a library, the basement which used to be a rec room he had insulated with sound blocking material then covered with dry wall to create an in-home theatre. His father rarely watched films.

While one room after another underwent a massive facelift the house was never the same in full for more than three months consecutive.

They sat in the kitchen at a marble top island both of them perched on high stools. His father poured wine from a chilled bottle; the father found it peculiar that his own son wore sunglasses during their brunch. The father had long since accepted that his son was an artistic type and that meant that certain things he found irregular were in fact regular for Charles. It was not for the father to understand but to accept and support, but irregular behavior more often than not suggested an unexamined influence and the father though suspect refused to give in to paranoia because paranoia thrived in the absence of trust, and so justification looked a hell of a lot like denial as the father put out thoughts of cocaine, heroin addiction or prescription drug abuse that might be influencing his son's strange behavior.

The father poured a glass of wine for his son.

Normally Charles was an active listener, he loved his father and he loved his father's stories. Charles and his father were not so unalike, they were both talented and personable, both had went down the wrong path from time to time; they were men that stayed the crooked course drinking and drugs and desperate women became a lifestyle that was never meant to be permanent, and if it got to be more a habit than a phase they both knew to make a stark U-turn back to the straight and narrow.

But his father's stories always seemed less insane by the standard of yesteryear, it seemed that in the late seventies and early eighties a man could get away with just about anything. Men could still be chauvinists, (whether better or worse), and drinking and drugs were still fun as America was just in the early stages of Regan and Bush Sr's campaigning to vilify mind altering substances.

But Charles hadn't gotten a goodnight sleep in over a week and it was getting harder to keep out the distractions in order to maintain polite conversation, sunglasses usually helped.

His father said, "I would be at the bar. I meant well, I mean, well, I was always at the bar all the time. And a friend of mine who was going through the same thing told me, 'You know, it took me about three years' and I said, 'Wow.' Three years seemed like such a long time."

Charles refilled his father's wine glass.

The father explained, "But you know, the damnedest thing, there were good times and there were hard times but in the end, it took about three years."

Charles finished his glass and poured himself another, under his breath he says, "*Three years.*"

Charles opened the front door of his father's house and their black Labrador raced to get out ahead of him.

Charles and the dog walked down the long driveway and took a right. Pax was a hyperactive dog even at the old age of nine years and walking her round the block of their gated community was the only thing that calmed her down. And it calmed Charles down as well. Their walks were an opportunity for Charles to remove himself from expectations, obligations or perceptions generated by other people. What does it matter what other people think, even to a man who lives an unconscionable, do-what-you-feel lifestyle? At one point or another, what other people think is the only thing that matters, and it is especially true in vulnerable times.

The neighborhood was empty, there were never many people out on the street and if the neighbors were ever in their backyards the tall bushes that separated the houses canceled a lot of that noise. Even the weather seemed better than it really was in that neighborhood on days when Charles and Pax walked around the block.

Charles stopped as Pax stopped, and they stood there for a second. Charles focused on a hole torn in the chain link fence that separated the neighborhood from several lanes of freeway. He looked back at Pax, who was bent at the hide legs unloading a massive, solid shaft of feces, and Charles thought, 'That seems appropriate.'

*

In the evening during a familiar tradition Charles and his mother were together at her house for dinner and drinks. In the sitting room Charles sank into the bright white fabric of a designer couch. His mother sat across from him on a matching couch; in appearance she could not have been more his opposite. Where he lay on the couch as upright as a blanket, his mother sat rigid as a wooden broomstick. Her makeup was impeccable while his hair and week old beard were dirty and matted. Her dress new and pristine, his shirt used and wrinkled—

They both enjoyed their scotch.

"You should really, I beg you to reconsider-- this."

Charles sat forward as if to better hear her, hoping that if he could hear her he could better understand what she was saying, he sipped his scotch and chewed on a piece of ice, he squinted at her indicating that she should elaborate. For a second without speaking his mother moved her hands as if she were a taffy-pull and then said with resistance,

"The-- way that-- you should reconsider... your life design. You should reconsider the way you *present* yourself."

Charles nods in a defiant way and leans back.

He finished his scotch and he looked at the ceiling. His mother's house has very high ceilings and he felt a sudden vertigo, as if there were a risk that whatever made gravity gravity could suddenly go in reverse and the high ceilings worried him because if the world were turned upside-down it would mean a long fall. As a child he often forgot his fear and would bolt straight up trees, charge up sheer cliffs and reach the summit of a welcome challenge full of excitement, high, pausing serine, taking in the view, and then ultimately come crashing back to reality, emotionally fucked by the fear, realizing he would have to work his way back down.

A third person's voice came from across the room,

"Dinner will be ready in a few minutes."

Charles rolled his head to a level position coming back to present day away from all those tall trees and steep dirt cliffs, looking from his mom to another woman standing in the doorway. She was composed like mother, but the same age as Charles. The woman smiled and held up a hand, her hand turned at the wrist waving at Charles. Charles smiled, and his mom looked confused,

"You remember Claire? She used to live down the street from us when we were still on Burton."

A moment passes, Charles smiles, Claire smiles too. His mother waits for an indication whether Charles remembers Claire or he just can't help but flirt with every woman he meets, because flirting is creating a false kind of familiarity in order to be intimate with strangers, and because Charles is attracted to Claire at that moment he is smart enough not to indicate whether or not he remembers her. Remembering her could mean one of two things, good or bad.

"It's good to see you, Charlie."

"You too, Claire."

Mom explains, “She's in school. She's a culinary genius. The super elite restaurants downtown are about to start a bidding war to hire her, she wanted a reference and so I offered to hire her as a personal chef. Just a few nights a week”

“Tonight we’re having Duck sautéed in orange sauce served with parmesan crusted truffles. It’s lovely, you’ll swear it is a little piece of heaven.”

Charles opens another bottle of scotch and admires Claire’s ankles. Mom asks again, “You do remember Claire?”

In the basement limited light comes in from the west side of the building, Claire walks on ahead, she walks in a crisscross pattern, one leg crosses the other, and her pencil skirt frames the contours of her hips and thighs. She unbuttons her blouse and throws it over a wardrobe.

Charles follows a few steps behind.

Claire unzips the side of her skirt and steps out of it; she lays it over the back of a chair. Charles follows her to a table between shelves of aged wine. Claire pulls off her underwear, steps out of them and then sits on a thick wooden workbench.

Her body is exceptional, charged and reserved, shapely but sharp. She stands there thinking about how she looked all those years ago naked in his room with the movie posters still hanging on the walls, all the T-shirts with logos, and how smooth his face was, how his thighs and chest were bald, and how nervous he used to get when he would steal a bottle of wine from his parents that they would sneak alone together, sipping red from the bottle back then, kissing, touching and undressing each other was just as good as sex itself.

Charles approaches her but stops just out of arms reach. He smiles and looks at the bottles of wine lining the shelves in his mother's cellar. Claire balls up her underwear and throws them at him.

"Were you lying?"

Charles catches her underwear in one hand. He smiles at her, says her name, takes a minute to enjoy the moment and still smiling says,

"Claire... I'll always remember you."

She draws her knees to her chest and crosses her arms over her legs, she tilts her chin low and looks at him from under her brow,

"I want it to be just like the first time."

Charles moves toward Claire sure not only that it will be like their first time, but far, far better, far deeper, considering how long it's been and how much they have grown.

*

Mr. Deprimere is a big man, not necessarily tall, not necessarily overweight, visually big, big like a pit-bull.

He sits behind a big oak desk in a small office, crème color blinds let in a soft light that gives the space a comforting warmth, visually, which is intentional. Like people, places are decorated to achieve an intended façade, visual warmth creates a sentimental atmosphere and when people are victim to their emotions they desire intimacy, validation, and this allows the highest caliber of personal admissions to flow.

Mr. Deprimere drinks his coffee while Charles ignores him.

Charles is slumped in a big leather executive chair and he plays with his lighter while Mr. Deprimere looks over a calendar, between sips of his coffee, "How was your weekend?" Mr. Deprimere asks.

Charles rolls his head a full circle, then again in a clockwise direction, "Spent it with my parents."

Mr. Deprimere stirs his coffee with a red straw, he watches Charles with an uncommitted smile,

"Anything to drink?"

"Oh, of course, gotta stay hydrated," Charles replies with two flicks of his lighter.

"That's not what I'm saying."

"Coffee. A lot of coffee goes a long way."

Mr. Deprimere holds up his mug, Charles holds up his lighter, and then with two fingers Mr. Deprimere taps the calendar open on his desk, "You've got a court date coming up. Are you going to impress them or just sit there like a teenage punk, like you do every time we've met so far?"

Charles throws his legs off the arm of the chair and leans forward, with his forearms on his knees Charles points the lighter at Mr. Deprimere, "I'm going to WOW..." and then leaning back and crossing his legs at the knee finishes, "...the pants off them."

Charles flicks his lighter twice.

Mr. Deprimere closes his calendar and he leans back in his own chair as he says,

“That's what I like to hear. I know you're thinking it's not going to get better, but it will. Sometimes it will get worse, but as long as you keep in mind, like I'm always saying, keep in mind what you're looking forward to, keep that in your focus, one thing at a time, it will keep your spirits up.”

Charles pushes his sunglasses back up to the bridge of his nose. He smiles to himself at the word *spirits.*

Mr. Deprimere says, “It's not one day at a time. It's the opposite.”

Charles nods and flicks his lighter three times as he stands, then gives a salute which leads into a bow, Charles then turns and makes to go out of the office.

Mr. Deprimere asks, “How did you get to my office this morning?” and Charles promises, with a smile that he didn’t drive there.

*

"Well, there's a lot about me you don't know for sure, but we just met, you're going to get the full story, possibly abridged, but the full story nonetheless, now what the fuck was I saying..."

Charles takes a second to get his bearings, and shouts over the music, "You were attacked." Brett nods and pushes her hair behind her ear while she jumps back warding off invisible opponents, her arms wave out of control and she enacts the moment, both herself at the instant of the attack as well as the movements of her attacker. Charles sips his drink without taking his eyes off her. Unlike most people he meets Charles is hooked on Brett. He is transported back to middle school, he's a total geek, he actually laughs at her jokes, he can't stop smiling. The girl is a riot.

"The second time, right..."

She jumps from one profile to the other to distinguish between herself and her attacker,

"Right. Well you wouldn't know it from looking at me, but I'm all fight, and broke-ass junkies who spot a five foot girl walking alone on an empty street who is going to take out your eyes if you fuck with me, is, is well, a surprise. So, I'm walking home from the gym..."

Brett is a train wreck, a wild child if there ever was one; she goes from standing to sitting to standing again within a minute.

"I'm full of adrenaline and all my senses are heightened, I get home, I get out of my car and like a dumbass I don't check both directions on the street where I live, because yeah, I'm fearless and I'll live in crack-town to save a couple bucks on rent, I hear him before I see him, and when I hear him coming up behind me I turn with a fist full of keys. I've got the keys between my fingers pointed out like claws."

Brett is a life enthusiast. She is literally wiped from one side of the room to another with and by any fleeting inspiration.

"I punch him in the face and cut into his cheek and his eye, and 'cause he can't see he's waving around this little pocket knife and it cuts me, real bad, there's blood everywhere and I'm feeling no pain..."

Brett and Charles, though alike in the lifestyle, are polar-opposite when it comes to their zeal.

She hands Charles another Manhattan and then lies across the couch, he is planted in the chaise end of the sectional.

Charles grabs her ankle with his free hand and begins to massage her foot and for a minute he wonders 'do all men know how to massage a woman's foot?' and if they do, did they learn massaging their mother's feet when they were young, which makes him wonder if that is strange.

Brett acknowledges the gesture but could care less, what's happening is less than thrilling and becomes boring. Life needs life, living from moment to moment means—

The song on her iPod changes and Brett is kick-started back to a state of living, she spins her hips, throws a leg over Charles and drops herself in his lap. "Have you ever heard the band Say Hi to Your Mom? Ah-- I never listen to this sad bastard shit, but it speaks to me, I really, really love it, it's exactly how I feel right now at this point in my life." With her teeth she rips a cigarette out of a nearly demolished pack, in the process almost biting through the filter. Charles flicks his lighter and she sticks the tip of her cigarette into the little blue flame, she apologizes in advance, "I'm on the last day of my cycle."

Brett is curled up on the couch with her head in Charles lap, "I hate her so much. Like I can't even tell you, my sister was my best friend, my whole life and..." and she cries for a long time before the good times begin again.

Brett lies naked in her bed; Charles stands over her as he buttons his shirt. She is in such a deep sleep that she doesn't move as Charles leans over to kiss her forehead. He stands there another second watching her breathe, as she inhales the tattoos on her lats expand, they rise and fall and Charles leaves.

*

It is early, not for most but early for most like Charles. He is nervous and unfamiliar with the feeling. For years Charles had been secure in who he was and what his purpose was, why he was the person he was and how he would maintain the person he was in order to improve the man he would be. For the last three weeks it was impossible for him to tell where he belonged. Being with a woman meant validation, meeting someone to talk with and have a drink with and wake up with meant the day wasn't a total waste.

Supposing life is just something that happens, the only evidence of living are the moments collected, memories as a child, moments with his mother, moments with his father, without events feelings and stories worth retelling, seconds, minutes and hours drag on with nothing to show. After high school and college the only thing to remember is the wedding, child birth and from its beginning the child's life becomes the reversal wherein the child's moments of accomplishment become our memories. But Charles was never meaning to get married. Charles was never out to produce offspring and raise them up to be respectable members of society. Marriage was unlikely because of the whole 'till death do us part.' And kids seemed unlikely, as Charles was no more mature than most adolescents. So what becomes of a man without purpose, whether a man achieves his goals or gives up on them? What else is there but to drink too much and meet women? How can you tell the difference between the seven days of the week? Charles had been a mess for nearly a month, and on this particular morning he felt inclined to make a motion in the direction of self-preservation, self-respect. Like his mother's request he meant to do something about *this.*

Charles stands outside the front door of Mr. Deprimere's building, chain-smoking cigarettes, and smiling at everyone as he holds the door for people coming and going. But mostly he's waiting because he doesn't have Mr. Deprimere's phone number, and he's trying to catch Mr. Deprimere as he arrives to work hoping that there will be a few free minutes before his first appointment in which they can talk.

Charles smokes another cigarette and starts to think Mr. Deprimere might not be coming into the office this morning just as he sees a car pull into the lot, Charles catches a glimpse of the driver's profile and Charles smiles to himself.

A minute later Mr. Deprimere is walking up the steps of the offices and Charles takes off his aviators to look into Mr. Deprimere's face.

"What are you doing here Charles?"

"Maybe hoping for a session."

"We're not scheduled till next Monday."

"Yeah, I thought maybe I could be a little more progressive in our meetings."

"That's great, I look forward to it. Not today though."

"No?"

"No... Charles if you feel you need someone to talk to on a whim, when you finally feel you want or if you need to talk I can get you a sponsor."

"Thanks Deprimere, not yet, not yet since I'm not in AA and I'm not looking to get sober. I just need to convince you I'm sober enough to pass our counseling sessions. We aren't friends, right?"

Charles backs down the steps, and then jogs to his car. Mr. Deprimere takes a second to wonder what just happened.

*

During a break from his cubicle Charles sneaks into the break room and eats a little bit from each lunch belonging to his coworkers, even though he isn't hungry.

*

In the modern world we have gods that inspire, guide and frighten our culture into the 'group think' that becomes *trend*, starting with money, television as a medium, the governments rule, the price of youth, millionaire advertising, fashion dictates, etc.

These are the gods that determine our future as mortals.

Charles flips through the new releases, though even before he stopped at Ameba he knew what he was there to buy.

Killing time he looked around to see if anything stood out, eventually he went straight to the letter S and pulled out a couple of albums by Say Hi to Your Mom.

"Charlie?"

He turned in the direction of the voice.

"Hey" she says, "It's Amy."

Charles sips from a Styrofoam cup and says *hey* back. She turns her head at an angle and shoots him a disapproving stare.

"Shut up, I know your name. I'm just surprised to see you."

"How have you been?" she asks.

"I'm good, unfortunately sober," and smiling he takes another drink.

Amy asks, "Is that just coffee?"

Charles looks into the Styrofoam cup and says, "It was when I bought it."

A lull in conversation, Charles takes an interest in being open, honest, he asks what is on his mind, "How is Duke?"

Amy smiles because up until Charles asking this she wasn't sure it was even worth saying hello when she spotted him walking down Sunset.

"He's good, but he's fat now."

"Are you still walking him at Runyon?"

"I am but he's so fat he basically quits after fifteen minutes. He sits and he stares at me and his eyes just shout *I'm over it, take me home*."

"I would probably do the same."

There is another lull but neither want to say goodbye because it has been years, so Amy like any normal person says what comes to mind, and without regard how it might sound asks, "Did I hear you and..."

"Isabel?"

"Broke up?"

"Yes."

"How are you doing?"

"Still good." Charles says as he takes a long pull from his Styrofoam cup. Amy smiles a crooked smile, throws her right hand around like she's picking words out of the air and says,

"If you ever want to have coffee, I mean... *coffee* coffee, let me know."

And for a moment there is no bullshit civility, no ambiguity, just a moment where two people are honest without subtext, without ulterior motives, a man and woman neither out to get laid or be in a relationship stand in a CD shop and they really see one another.

Charles says, "I don't have your number anymore."

Amy contorts her face projecting skepticism and says, "I'm sure you'll figure out how to contact me," she touches his cheek and says, "Be well, handsome."

Then it's over, at least it seems and she turns away from him as if to leave, but then she turns back and throws her arms around Charles, hugging him, she rests her cheek against his chest.

Charles stands there with his arms out at shoulder level, one hand holding his drink the other gripped to a short stack of CDs. He stands there awkward as if Amy is covered in mud. He is too confused by the moment to think to hug her back.

Pulling away she says, "You motherfucker, you smell exactly the same as you did in high school. UGH. That smell is like Spanish Fly." She then jumps a foot back, releases him and without looking back and heads out past the long line of people waiting to check out.

Charles stands there frozen, both arms out in the exact position as the instant that Amy lunged at him, with his arms up high around his shoulders with a drink in one hand and a stack of CDs in the other, he only moves to lift his right arm higher and take a long drag from the crook of his shoulder.

*

Like a room that simply would not accept the furniture that inhabits it, Charles could not ease his mind of things to do. He thought about jogging, but he didn't know where his running shoes were packed away. He thought about writing some new material, and yet he didn't have the courage to branch out. He thought about a million things he should do, but he was still the same man, and what a little moonlight can do deserves its due respect, but moonlight in a man's heart can only do so much to improve him, not change him. So like a young couple in their first apartment he alone moved furniture from one side of the room to another: find shoes, go jogging, write new poems-- keep good, trash bad. What the Feng Shui in Charles life needed was a massive overhaul.

Pax breathes heavy and coarse before they make it even half way around the block. The dog keeps her head low to the ground, lower than her shoulders. Her tongue hangs out; the front of her back paws drag slightly as she moves her hind legs to keep up. At one of the first checkups after they brought Pax home the veterinarian explained that she would suffer increased pain from hip dysphasia, as she got older. The dog loved to run, despite the pain in her back legs and she was a good runner. Most days Charles and Pax went around the block just once, since she had gotten older it was clear if she went too far the pain would last for hours after. Pax breathes heavy and her head hangs low, she pants but she's smiling.

Charles and Pax make it around the block, they stop in front of his father's house; they look at each other for a second and then they both sit down in the grass under a eucalyptus tree.

*

'Anyone over the age of sixteen who isn't a college student or homeless that still goes to the library, they are a special kind of people,' Charles thinks to himself standing at a desk in the Beverly Hills library as he signs a waiting list to use the internet.

The people that surround him seem to have no place to be, no other place to go, killing time between days, sometimes reading, sometimes sleeping; a world of knowledge during business hours serves better as a halfway house than an institution for learning. Where people read John Grisham and people loan out Adam Sandler films, Ambrose Bierce goes years sitting on the shelf, Leonard Cohen CDs never listened to. Libraries are one of America's finest endangered species.

Charles sits at the first free computer. He sets out his cell phone and takes note of the time as he starts. He creates a new email and types,

The town decorates on Friday nights,

Even with no one watching he's nervous and he types,

They cover the walls with shit and the streets flood with piss.

It used to be he wrote like a bull and throwing his weight at the keyboard he would plow through words,

It's sickening but it's still more fun than my last stay in Hell.

Charles reads the poem and then deletes it.

Ten minutes go by and he's written and deleted five more poems. He leans back, crosses his arms and rubs at the short hair under his chin. His cell phone vibrates and Charles jumps at it. He plays stenographer as the voice asks,

Is it true?

Charles whispers into the cell phone, still typing,

It is.

So... what are you going to do now?

I'm kind of living out of my car. I'm staying with friends. I might travel. I don't know.

So—

Pause.

Should we meet?

Well, every time I was single you were with someone, and you know, the other way around.

We could meet.

How about we meet half way?

Hmmm.

The timing is never going to be more perfect.

They pause a moment. Charles is more in the writing than in the conversation. He considers if it's material. He reads it and then deletes it.

"Are you still there?"

Charles begins to answer just as he gets another call. Looking at the caller ID, it reads: Brett.

Charles answers suddenly, "Hang on Liza, I've got another call, can I call you back?"

As he hangs up, she rushes to say "Okay, but wait, I can get tomorrow and Wednesday off if you want to--"

"I'll call you back, I'll call you back," Charles hangs up on Liza to answer Brett's call. Charles sits forward, enthusiastic for the first time in days. He says *Hey* and really means it.

Brett says, "You disappeared."

"Didn't you get my text?"

"Oh yeah, for sure."

"What's up?"

"I don't know, nothing."

"I'm here, you have my number."

"You didn't disappear?"

"NO. I fell head over heels for this wild child, and I figured I'd drop off the grid and wait to hear back from her."

There is convincing laughter here. She says, "Oh, my God you crack me up."

"I'm glad my pain is worth something. I kept driving past your house with a ghetto blaster and a Peter Gabriel cassette, and then I never stopped because I remembered you were probably hung-over and that would just annoy the piss out of you."

"Oh my God, you're so funny."

Charles puts his free hand to his temple, "So what's up?"

"Nothing. How about you?"

Charles asks, "You want to hang out tomorrow night?"

"I shouldn't, I've got work in the morning."

Charles rubs at his shoulder and then at the back of his neck, "Alright, well, give me a call when you get tired of making everything you say super vague."

Charles ends the call and is awash with rage, confusion and regret. He grinds his teeth. Ultimately he is proud but he hates that he can't get a hold of the things he is feeling. He doesn't want to be owned by his emotions, he hates that his breathing is irregular and that the hairs on his arms stand up, and he is afraid that if he tried to speak his voice would falter. A middle-aged man working at the computer next to Charles looks over. They exchange a glance. The middle-aged man directs his gaze over at a sign that says: No Cell Phones. The middle-aged man gives Charles a second dirty look. Charles leans over and presses down the power button on the middle-aged man's computer.

"Asshole," the old man mumbles.

Charles' phone vibrates; he opens the phone and puts it to his ear.

"What the fuck was that?" she asks.

Charles lowers the volume of his voice, "I'm sorry. I can't get comfortable around people who act so noncommittal. Everything they say is, like, begging to be interpreted. Brett, if you want to hang out just say something, anything, say one direct thing."

Her voice changes her, not by much, she remains cool but she speaks in a calm authoritative way, "Hanging out would be very nice, but I can't tomorrow. I have a ton of work to finish..."

Charles takes the phone away from his ear, holds it at an arm's length and whispers to himself, "That speaks volumes." He puts the phone back to his ear and Brett is still talking, "...and I thought it would be better to put my work off till a night when I knew I needed to get to bed at a reasonable hour without drinking my face off."

Having accomplished nothing, Charles says, "You're right. Thank you for being direct. I'm not that guy, I just don't have the patience or resources. I want people to have exactly what they want."

Pause.

"Charlie, I don't think you're that guy."

Pause.

She asks, "Are we cool?" and Charles answers, "Super cool." He hangs up the phone and a librarian tells him "Sir, your time is up."

They had met through the internet, which many people do, but their story was unique in that neither of them had the intention of 'meeting singles.' Charles' Mother was on weekend in San Francisco with some friends and was at a craft show and she ran into a girl named Liza. Somehow it came up that this Liza knew Charles, she and Charles' mother spoke briefly about him and when their conversation ran its course and they said their goodbyes this girl named Liza told Charles' mother to inform him of 'the wedding'. When the details of this were recounted to Charles he couldn't figure out who the girl was. And having nothing to go on but the name Liza and 'a wedding' and that she worked somewhere in San Francisco he went on the Internet and stalked. He found a woman in the right vicinity and her profile photo was from a wedding. After the extensive search and half a bottle of Wild Turkey he sent her a message congratulating her on the wedding and when she replied to the email she wrote "I'm not sure I know who you are." And so initiated a yearlong communication in which they wrote one another, sometimes intimately, but mostly they exchanged adages, advice and perspective on the problems that occurred in each other's lives. There was a freedom in telling about troubles with dating, career woes and what it all meant that they were nearing thirty. Sharing these personal things with a friend they had never met and could not judge or be judged by was liberating. While the one was in a relationship often the other was single and they took turns trying to convince the other to meet, but they were respectful people, and they respected the people they were committed to. There was a lot to say between smart, considerate kindred spirits. And so they were always in touch.

It was one straight shot up the 5, thinking of nothing Charles drove straight through. With his left leg bent up against his chest and one hand hanging loosely on the wheel he smoked cigarettes, drank, refilled and drank again from his Styrofoam cup. He eased off the accelerate as he passed highway patrol; all the while listening to *Discosadness* back to back. He hadn't thought much about seeing Amy when buying CDs, not till that moment when he was an hour out of the city and so he decided when he got back to Los Angeles he would have to seek out her contact info.

The road was defined by nothing, out of focus, anything beyond twenty feet in front of his car was blurred, marked by nothing, meaning nothing and gone as quickly in the same moment that it sped into sight. Charles' rationalization was that bad drivers can't drive drunk, and bad drunks can't drive, Charles believed that the reason people drive like retards with a few in them was because people don't understand the drink. Because alcohol relaxes people it immediately makes them a hazard on the road, and because alcohol slows down a person's reaction time they forget that they are navigating a three thousand plus hunk of machinery propelling at anywhere from thirty to ninety miles an hour and at any isolated second that they look away from the road could mean disaster. A second for a drunk in reality is more equal to five—which means texting, picking out a CD, pouring a drink, any menial task could take a man's life while drunk driving. Focus, be alert, never take your eyes off the road. Charles repeats this to himself and then explains in his head to an imaginary audience that might judge him that this was not to be meant as advice for the inebriated motorist as most drivers are idiots and most drunks are irresponsible.

No, focus, be alert and never take your eyes from the road, these were words to live by at any given moment of our waking life.

For hours, the only place Charles looked was straight ahead or to his smokes to light another cigarette, smoke raced from the little orange ember as he inhaled, at a moment in his lungs was then pulled through the open window and it escaped the car, it disappeared into nothing somewhere out on the freeway.

Barefoot, Charles walks into the lobby of a hotel. Lost and disoriented he looks in both directions before finding a hotel clerk, safe behind the check-in desk the young girl watches him carefully as Charles has been making her increasingly nervous since the moment he sped into the parking lot. The girl is still unsure whether or not he is a threat. Charles salutes her and approaches the counter.

The clerk says, "Good evening," and Charles smiles politely, "Good evening."

"I made reservations a few hours ago."

"Charles Kazmar?" she says it with a hint of recognition, but she isn't sure she recognizes him as he hasn't taken off his sunglasses.

"Just Charles, or Chuck, anything but my full name."

"Charlie?"

"That will do."

"One bed, for the fifth and the sixth?"

For the first time hearing the date it sounds familiar, but he isn't sure why.

"Wait, shit, tomorrow's the sixth?"

"Mhmm."

"Scratch the second night. I've got to get back tomorrow."

"What brings you to Lost Hills?"

"Seriously? Lost Hills? Huh. Um... it's... uh, half the distance between my home town and the home town of an Internet *pen pal*."

Here the girl adapts a more professional attitude and hands him a small envelope, "Your keys. If you need anything dial 0."

In the second floor hallway Charles bangs a bellhop kart against the door jam. In order to bring in the things he didn't trust to leave in the car Charles collected them on a bellhop kart. He managed to get it on the elevator but finds himself stuck in the upstairs hallway with the kart sideways turning it this way and that like a teenager learning to parallel park. He pauses a second, his eyes still hidden by his aviators. Taking a moment he looks at the bellhop kart stuck sideways in the hallway and he sips from his Styrofoam cup. Charles knows there is a simple, uncomplicated solution to this moment of insanity and he smirks. Mostly he just likes that he's alone, drunk in a hotel hallway banging a bellhop kart between two walls.

He holds his Styrofoam cup between his teeth and gets his hands on the bellhop kart, beginning again, shoving it this way and that.

Minutes later inside his hotel room Charles pours three fingers of Whiskey in his Styrofoam cup.

TWENTY-NINE

Minutes later, Charles hooks up his computer, plugs in an iPod and fills the hotel room with loud harmonies.

Minutes later Charles pinches an unlit cigarette between his teeth and uses scissors to trim his pubic hair over the bathroom sink.

Charles is hiking up a small dirt hill. There is no grass, and the trees are as dry as the earth. When he gets to the top he looks out over the town and there is nothing, nothing but trees and dry earth. No fast food shops or strip malls. There are plants and water towers, the power lines are scarce. Charles lights a bowl. The sky is gray, thick with clouds and it seems to enclose the town. Charles holds the smoke in his lungs and wonders where everyone is, how it is there is so little civilization, and then he exhales, long and labored and he heads back.

As Charles comes down the hill, he stops near the freeway, as the cars fly by, he looks up stoned, transfixed and confused by a WRONG WAY sign.

He stands there another minute and then walks toward the hotel.

Loud music plays from an otherwise empty wing of the hotel. Twenty feet from his room the second floor overlooks the front lobby.

Charles gets a text that says: I'm here.

He does his best to hide in the open hallway, he carefully inspects guests of the hotel from a distance. A little old man checks in, Charles hides around the corner. A little old lady meanders as if she is looking for someone. Charles gets nervous and hides out of sight as he swallows the whiskey in his Styrofoam cup.

The sound of an elevator chime has Charles turn to his right. As he looks up the length of a wine colored carpet a tall woman walks towards him.

"Lars?" she says.

"Oh my God, I'm glad you're you. I saw that decrepit old woman at first and I panicked. I had no idea what I'd do if it turned out that the old woman was you."

"What?"

"You know those stories about people creating false identities to impress people... um, on the internet... and then people think they have these amazing connections with people who don't really even exist."

"I'm me."

Charles smiles broadly, "You're taller than I expected."

"I told you I was tall."

"I guess, but I couldn't really tell from pictures."

"I could tell you were tall."

"I guess I don't think about those things until I'm face to face."

"Like how you smell or the way you taste."

"I had to shower so I might smell like hotel soap and--"

Liza buries her nose in Charlie's chest.

She says, "Oh, my God. I'm in trouble."

Liza sits on the bed while Charles pours two drinks.

"There's nothing around here."

"That's ridiculous."

"Like nothing. I drove around for a while because the directions said to go left when it was a right as soon as you get off on the exit. I kept expecting it to break into a major street where there'd be any kind of restaurant. But there was nothing."

"We should have tried that bar."

"That bar was a barn."

They laugh and when they sip the whiskey they lock eyes.

Liza says, “I grew up in an area like this. The sticks aren't that bad.”

“I get that it's not a big deal for a couple days. But in case I want to see a movie or buy a book or eat something that isn't fried in bacon fat, honkys can keep this shit.”

“You're funny, Lars.”

“Yeah.”

“I've never drank straight whiskey before. You know I usually need a mixer or a beer to wash it down.”

He looks at her where she is perched on the edge of the bed while he is standing. Charles takes Liza’s hand by the wrist and kisses her palm then he kisses her on the cheek and puts her hand in his jeans. They smile and kiss gently and undress, they get under the sheets and Charles grabs her under the knees and wraps her legs around him, they begin to move gently, she turns her head when he tries to kiss her mouth, and Charles watches her, her eyes shut, she won’t open her eyes, Charles backs up and turns Liza over on her belly, she pushes herself against him and he tries to get inside her but he looks confused,

"What's up?"

"I'm not sure."

"You okay?"

"I'm fine."

"That happen a lot?"

"Never."

"Thanks. It's okay. "

Liza turns onto her back propped up on her elbows, her perfect breasts lay idly on display as she says, "Let's get something to eat."

Charles takes out a twenty and sets his wallet next to the bottle of whiskey near the TV. While Charles pays the deliveryman

Liza picks up his wallet to look at his driver's license expecting to have a laugh at his picture.

The room is a mess, except for the bed every piece of furniture is turned over, garbage from the takeout liters the bed and after a long quiet moment Liza asks,

"Why would you tell me your name was *Lars*?"

"In case you ever called."

"What do you mean? We talked all the time?"

"I was with Isabel for five years. Before her I always ran around on girls if we were fighting or it seemed like we were going to split up. With Isabel I was a good boy, I never cheated on her, not once, but when her and I fought I had you. I don't know if it was disloyal or dishonest. It just seemed safer if you didn't know who I really was."

"Charles Kazmar?"

"Yeah?"

"The Charles Kazmar? I've only heard about you, even though we've known each other, which is weird. I have a friend who loves your stuff, I don't really know. But that's you?"

"Mhmm."

"You're so weird."

"Yeah."

"But you smell so good."

"I'm pretty good in the sack... too… normally."

And here she laughs hysterically.

Charles comes out of the hotel room with a towel around his waist and has his cell phone to his ear. He whispers into the phone as he looks in both directions of the hallway. Brett talks as if she is uninterested in life, she is flippant and it frustrates Charles; yet he can't help slamming the brakes, he wants to throw his life to a screeching halt at anything potential with Brett.

"Yeah, I can talk," though his voice is obstinate.

"Want to get a drink?" which she asks as if she were speaking to a handbag. EX: 'I'm going out, handbag, are you coming with me?'

And Charles isn't sure what to say.

Liza and Charles were asleep for a few hours, they had passed out in their room a few hours ago. They ran out of whiskey and smoked a little, then after awhile they fell asleep, dead to the world with their arms around each other. That's when Brett called.

Charles looks at his feet, "I can't right now."

"I'm so tired and I can't sleep."

Frustrated by Brett's unresponsive nature as she is the one that called him at two in the morning Charles spits out, "Roll on your stomach and shove your face in the pillow."

"Would you be happier if I was dead?"

He had meant the comment to seem sexual in nature, as in *lay on your belly and finger your clit*, but she didn't follow.

"No one killed themselves with a pillow."

"I need to get more cigarettes. I'm going insane. I drank way too much and totally forgot to buy smokes."

Charles puts an arm on the sharply textured wallpaper, he leans on the corner of the wall outside his hotel room and under his breath he says, "My heart is breaking for you."

"Why are you whispering?"

"I told you I can't get away."

"If you can't talk, that's fine."

"Don't give me that. I asked you out tonight, and you fucking told me you needed to stay home and work."

"Fine."

"No, it's not fine. Do you have any idea of what *fine* really means--"

When Brett doesn't reply Charles looks at his phone and says, "Fuck."

TWENTY-NINE

She’s hung up. Charles closes his phone.

TWENTY-NINE

Pt. II

TWENTY-NINE

Through the windshield miles go by in silence. There is no light except out ahead from the headlights of Charles car, yellow reflectors maintain the width of the freeway, the freeway lines maintain Charles, he blinks through black spots in his consciousness, the wheel and the radio and the road turn into nothing, black spots are empty, no dreaming, no thoughts about anger or better times.

Miles of silence lend themselves to the hours spent waiting

Charles and Amy walk the streets of an art festival. The sky is bright and vivid and the red bricks of the neighboring buildings make the world seem color corrected. People were friendlier then; Charles and Amy were lovers, close, considerate, though not head-over-heels, their feet were well grounded even if their heads were in the clouds. Charles leans in and almost kisses Amy, she turns and laughs. When she tries to kiss him he turns the same.

I love running and I hate goodbyes; I wish I had somewhere to go

In a rest stop parking lot, the first thing, the only indication that Charles is still alive is a flicker of the eyelids. His eyes adjust, and he tries to focus on the dome light. He turns to his left and his eyes peek out from the driver's side window. He begins to rise slowly, his body is stiff from falling asleep in the car. He looks over at the sunrise and wonders how far he has to get back.

I think people are rude by nature but our culture thinks otherwise

"Most men's better days don't hold a candle to the biography I'm living," Charles reads from a spiral bound notebook and then drags on his cigarette. Charles sits on a stage and to his side hangs a microphone fixed to a stand, Charles pauses because he knows that they are waiting, and people love the wait.

"It's time to grow fangs and hunt in the night--"

A beer and a shot sit on a stool next to Charles.

"--Sleep is for suckers."

Charles turns the page and the audience roars with applause. A sea of rowdy drunken people fill the bar and they gather in front of the stage. Charles gives half a smile and sips his beer.

A thin, scantily dressed girl sewn together with mascara and cheap perfume shouts, "CHUCK! Read SOMETHING SEXY!"

And the rowdy drunken audience roars with applause. Charles squints in the direction of the voice because the lights are in his eyes and it is hard to see faces in the crowd. He sips his beer,

"Oh, great," he wants to see her face, but it's enough to know she can see his, "We've got a sex addict in the crowd. That's a first."

And the audience cheers their rowdy drunken applause.

Charles sips his beer and shrugs to another side of the crowd, "Why would anyone shout lick my cerebral clit when they're in a crowded place like this. Just depraved. Degenerate sex junkies," he smiles.

"FUCK YOU, CHUCK!" the girl shouts back. This makes Charles laugh, big and genuine, he tries to get a hold of it, it is a large laugh but it is humble. Charles is surprised by the sound even though it's a laugh he recognizes, it seems so long since he's heard it.

He squints in the direction of the girl's voice, "Fuck me? Is that all this is for you? What do you expect for your ten dollar admission?"

Charles drinks his shot and chugs his beer, a few cheers from people in the audience, and Charles wipes his chin, he says it like its to the girl but she's part of the past now, "You'll have to get in line and hope it still works."

The girl shouts, "SUCK MY DICK, CHUCK!"

And the audience laughs, and Charles laughs too. He opens his spiral notebook to a new page.

"Oh, well if she's got a dirty mouth, dogs keep away from that woman. That sex offender is mine tonight--"

Cheers persist.

"Now enough courting. Where was I, oh, yeah, I was just about to read *Something Sexy* for my friend with the dirty mouth."

*

And then Charles is back at work staring at his computer monitor, as if nothing ever happened. He is sending a text message; that morning he had over slept and missed his session with Mr. Deprimere.

The Twat walks past his cubicle and notices Charles using his phone, just to be a part of the moment Charles' coworker to which he refers to as The Twat says, "I'm sorry I missed your standup thing."

Charles doesn't look up from his phone, his thumbs move slowly and he says, "It's not funny," he looks up and says, "It's not a big thing."

The Twat says, "I'll be at the next one for sure." And Charles says, "Really, don't trouble yourself."

The Twat leans back as if shocked that Charles would say something borderline rude. To cement his point Charles adds, "It's not your thing, and you weren't invited."

The Twat rubs at the fat under his chin and says, "Why don't you just bleed and get it over with, so you can be a man again." The Twat laughs and laughs, tickled, proudly he says, "I saw one of them country boy comedians say that last night and I just couldn't wait to say it in conversation. Hot damn, *just bleed and get it over with*." He rubs at his eyes.

Charles looks down at his hands; unconsciously he has linked three paperclips into a short chain and he is about to link a fourth. The Twat sighs contended and says, "Cool. It's five. See you tomorrow."

Kneeling on a sofa Charles and Cynthia kiss passionately, putting their hands on each other's neck, their tongues are out. Charles undoes the buttons on her shirt while she undoes the buttons on his. Her face is streaked with black mascara and her perfume makes him sick to his stomach. They pull off their tops and their skin smacks together squeezing each other's bodies tighter, closer.

In the bedroom Diane pushes Charles onto the bed, when he tries to sit up she puts a hand on his face and forces his head back because he is slightly drunk he falls back onto the bed. She pulls off his jeans, he grabs her by the hair and pulls her mouth to his, and they lock jaws almost biting each other while she makes a fist around his cock.

Charles is on his knees, Jessie has her skirt up around her waist, her chest and face are pressed against the wall of the elevator while Charles goes down on her, he has his fingers inside her, and she wants to scream, she never wanted to scream louder for longer, not more than that moment. The elevator goes from one floor to the next reaching its destination too soon.

Charles is on top of her, driving away, long, slow, powerful thrusts, her crotch elevates reaching towards him her hips force herself closer and closer and the insides of her thighs are taut and shaking. Kiera is blindfolded and so close to climax that she looks insane, her face looks agonized, like she's running with every muscle in her body and every will in her spirit she's running; not away, finally for one fleeting moment she isn't running away, she is running towards something, and when she hits that finish line she is aghast, she is sweating and upset and has lost all her rhythm, she's nervous-strong and she wraps her arms and legs around Charles as tightly as she can. Because of the blindfold she can't see his face despite her beauty and enthusiasm he looks bored.

Charles walks Pax down the driveway and they take a left.

They walk together saying nothing, but from time to time Pax looks up at him. Charles wears his aviator sunglasses to hide his eyes. When Pax looks up at Charles, Charles smiles and says, 'Good girl.'

So much of life is something that need not be complicated.

Walking Pax is simple because they are alone, but not lonely. He feels better, for a minute, and then he sees that hole. Charles stands there a second watching the freeway through the hole in the chain link fence that separates the residential area from the traffic. Then Pax pulls on her leash.

*

TWENTY-NINE

A moments rest from flirting, fighting or fucking finds Charles on a bench in a park enjoying conversation with Amy; while she's drinking coffee from an insulated mug he is drinking from his famous Styrofoam cup.

The air is clear and crisp; it's early before the sun breaks through the AM cloud cover. Los Angeles buzzes from the morning commute of the employed; it's still sane as all the local craziness, the homeless, the drifters and the dependents are still tucked away scrapping together some kind of rest. Without the madness the city seems functioning.

Amy looks beautiful in the morning. Her complexion is soft because she is a natural beauty, in the nighttime she adorns high fashion, and paints herself with exquisite designer makeup. Void of her night style seeing her in the morning before she's finished her coffee, with her scarf and big dark glasses she looks different but equally beautiful.

On the ground at their feet lies a fat old pug named Duke.

"It's really uncomfortable being half naked, in six inch heels and asked to look natural, naturally, and don't pose, but make your body interesting. You ever had to do that?"

Charles tilts his head down and looks over his sunglasses, "What?"

"Have you ever had to impress someone?"

Charles takes out a flask and freshens his drink, "I must have," he screws the top of his flask shut, leans forward and pets Duke's head. The pug looks up and it makes Charles smile.

"So you get paid and then you have all this money and it's like none of that indignity or getting over that inhibition ever mattered, till I have to wait and wait and wait for the next job and go through it all again."

Charles looks out at the city, it's early and there is very little smog, but there is still no sun, only clouds and the sound of the 101 on their left. Charles swallows a mouth full of whiskey and says,

“You get the photos out of it, though. People think you're pretty and you'll be able to look back at your life and say that's what I looked like when I was younger.”

Amy looks at Charles and she likes being there. It reminds her of why they stayed friends even after so much time had passed. He goes on,

“Even if it's a bullshit job wearing some stupid fucking bust adorned with peacock feathers with your tits out, it's still you.”

This makes her smile, she forgot that he could be charming, that he was a man of good character and he says,

“It's what you looked like at that moment.”

She is happy to be there, this ray of personality, this moment with the old Charles means he is happy too,

“Actually with peacock feathers that sounds like an awesome outfit.”

“Yeah, It does sound pretty awesome.”

Amy takes out her cell phone but she isn't getting a call, she holds up the cell phone and aims it at Charles. She snaps his picture. She took the photo to remember this moment, but when she looks at it, her brow furrows and she says, "You look terrible, you know."

A long time passes before either speaks. Amy closes her phone and sips her coffee. Charles drinks from his Styrofoam cup and looks out at the city.

Finally without looking at her he says, "I feel terrible."

*

Dehydrated and disoriented Charles wakes in his mother's living room, he crawls back up onto the couch, rolls on his back stares up at the high ceiling and names begin appearing in the white paint: Kathryn, Joleen, Elena, Jenny, Brett, Liza, Amy, Diane, Cynthia, Kiera, Jillian, Kerry, Nicky, Danni, Brynne, Leslie, Lily, Catlyn, Jamie and, and there were others, but—how many were there? Ten or more?

*

TWENTY-NINE

Charles drops a small nugget of cocaine on the fleshy muscle between his thumb and forefinger. He crushes it, he snorts it, then dumps another bump and takes it up the other nostril. He brushes under his nose, then gets out of his car, locks the door and walks through the small parking lot.

The red leather of the chair reminds Charles of when he was young. His father's home office had big leather furniture. The windows of his office faced west and in the evenings Charles and his father sat at the desk of his home office and watched the sun burn the sky a warm orange, and the sun itself burned brighter than anything Charles remembers ever seeing. Even at seven he understood that that office was a solace for his father, and that solace was a place Charles was invited every evening as the sun set, and that tradition was just for the men. At that age it felt like a boys club, something special and precious that a father wanted to share with no one else except his son, but he couldn't have understood at that time why that solace was off limits to his mother. What it was, was the father's solace away, anyplace away from the mother. For years Charles insisted he was not a child of divorce; he was a child, and his parents happened to be divorced. While the rest of a culture with parents that split up was defined by this trait, Charles was just a kid who happened to spend his time divided by two different homes.

Mr. Deprimere is back to his calendar because Charles is opting out of a reciprocated dialogue. Charles happens to remember things about his childhood in fleeting moments, not in a sentimental way, but superficial, seeing the brass fasteners on an office chair reminds him of sunsets with his father and now looking back he knows that his parents were already separated at that point, still living in the same house, and it wasn't till years later that when his parents fess up to Charles that the family was going to divide; and unlike the house or the boat or the furniture, neither parent would pick him, that neither would assume the full responsibility for Charles, but that he would be handed back and forth at their convenience. This sudden realization seems to mean something and instead of examining it further Charles admits this flashback holds deep and vested meaning, admitting this, then the thought is gone from his focus.

TWENTY-NINE

Everything means something; *get over it* Charles thinks to himself.

Mr. Deprimere says, "I was under the impression you wanted to be more proactive in these sessions."

"I changed my mind."

Disapproving, Mr. Deprimere says, "Something tells me something changed your mind."

The office reminds Charles of a thousand things, a thousand unspoken things that he can't put into words. A girl that he liked more than he let on, (which could be any girl as he liked them all for one reason or another) once explained to Charles that her very first art teacher taught her never, under no circumstance to sketch an image from a photo because there are rules upon rules that deem it unforgiveable, she explained with her words (as well as her hands) that to imitate someone else's style is one thing but to imitate someone's art is bad taste. She was a junky for Jim Henson's work from the children's programming to the macabre, and so a lot of her art showed his influence, she explained that for this piece I wanted to allude to the personalities of his work, but I was in no way intending to recreate or infringe on it. She loved Henson and she wanted to explore his mind by creating a piece that mimics his identity, art is art and there is very little room for invention, so know your creative roots and wear them proudly as you create your own exhibition, she said also the problem with drawing from a photo is that it limits creative interpretation, if an artist creates a still life it is a representation of reality fused with their perception of the model, but sketching from a photo creates a double perception, an unintended fracture in the view of its subject.

"Maybe I'm just a flag, you know, or a vessel that flows negative or positive. You ever change your mind on something?" Charles asks.

Mr. Deprimere nods, "I do. But when I notice a change in myself I look at the things around me, I look at the people in my life and I ask myself *are any of these things influencing my outlook*."

"So *who* has changed my mood?"

"Well now, you'd have to talk to me, tell me something about your life before I can offer counsel there by fulfilling my duty as your court appointed *counselor*."

Charles is wondering why it matters. Mr. Deprimere is a man the same as any, and as any man born of woman is on a journey, his success on that journey is based on his ambition, his character, and mostly what matters is that he maintains a good standing with the mighty four winds that direct the course of our lives. Nothing is predetermined or otherwise Charles couldn't be pissing it away, because he is convinced that this life is his to shape, what kind of a person, or a God would suggest that a man's destiny is an immovable certainty thereby convicting Charles to a life of drudging up flashes of charm in an otherwise shitty apathetic state, never in time enough to be genuine, to be of moral standing, for Charles the unfortunate nature of the beast is that we cannot all be great leaders of men. The thought that everything is set out for us makes a man lazy, it gives him little reason to go out and shape the world, philosophy and religion meet in an angry fuck session where nothing is settled. Charles wonders what Mr. Deprimere really thinks is the cause of all this, and why he won't settle for the fact that going through a major breakup is in fact a big fucking deal, that no matter how calm and disaffected a man acts when he's been with one woman, committed fully, in love and in lust, (perhaps not imagining a life that leads to marriage and kids but inevitably marches towards it), as the deadly clock that ticks loudly in every man's ear, there is no one place to stand, the world is a treadmill, everything a man does and every moment a man chooses to live or lay on the couch the great conveyor belt brings us moment by moment, hour by hour, closer to growing up or giving in.

Mr. Deprimere asks, "Why did you say *who* and not *what*?"

"Excuse me?" Charles looks up from his cuticles.

"*Who* has changed your mood?" Mr. Deprimere asks as he leans back in his chair.

Brett nods and pushes her hair behind her ear while she jumps back warding off invisible opponents, her arms wave out of control and she enacts both herself at the moment of attack as well as the movements of her attacker.

"Have you spoken with Isabel yet?"

"Nope... And that's not it."

"Is that true or is that just more teenage attitude?"

"Both."

"How was your weekend?"

"Awesome. I was drunk two days straight, I must have slept with five different women. Sounds awesome right? Every boy's dream?"

"If it makes you happy. Unless you're in a program that's trying to rehabilitate your--"

"I'm not in need of rehabilitation."

"You're an addict, maybe not drugs, but alcohol. People don't drink like--"

"I did a line of coke before I came in here. You know how often I do coke? Once a week, and only before we meet. So you can see me sober. Does that sound like an addict? I can't fucking afford coke, but I know if I do a bump before our sessions I'm alert and functional. See? That's control. Addicts don't have control over their life."

Charles didn't want a predetermined life, he wanted to go out into the world and spike his veins with impulse, he didn't want to be another sketch of a man, he didn't want to live in the shadow of millions of generations of better song, poetry, and novelist writers, or real minded people like doctors of science and philosophy. Everyman before him that grabbed a little bit of history and culture and made a name for himself, if he could never measure up to all those men celebrated like Gods, he would never become a household name, never more than the sum of his parts. Becoming a sketch of a photograph, of a sketch of a photograph, like two mirrors held up to one another, was his only option—other than to drink to excess, take no initiative whatsoever and let life be unaffected by him and vice versa.

Mr. Deprimere asks, "Are you in control of your life?"

"I'm the fucking writer, director, actor, grip, editor, and audience. I'm in control over my life, and I'm living it. You sit there at your desk leaned over like you're ready to jump into my skin and be me for an hour to know what real sex feels like, what a drink really tastes like, I fucking live in control over myself because I let people do whatever they want and I can be free to sit in the corner drunk or high or whatever, fuck girls if they want to or not fuck them, it's about what they want, I've never had to guilt someone into fucking me, I've never had to ask, take a look at every relationship where sex is power, and tell me who is the monster. I only sleep when there's nothing left to drink. I'm not like you; I don't want anything so I can have anything."

"That's nihilism."

Charles is upset for the first time in weeks, "I am what I do. You ever been to a poetry reading? It's a sad tissue fuck of emotional assholes begging people to say 'good job, wow, your inner light is such a warm blanket.' When I read people scream. When I read to an audience girls go home and fuck their boyfriends because they wish it was me. You know what I write about?"

"I have an idea."

"You think you do. But if you'd ever read my stuff you'd have put your hands up and said *no way* the moment my file landed on your desk."

"You want to read one for me?"

"How about you read one to your wife and if you get fucked tonight we agree I don't need rehabilitation."

"And you always do narcotics before you come into my office?"

"Since the day we met."

"I can have you tested for drugs."

"Yeah, but then I won't suggest the good stuff to get your wife off."

"Mention my wife again and I'll be forced to tell the judge exactly what I have assessed about you."

"Is this the part where I ask what your assessment is?"

"This is the part where you chill the fuck out and tell me why you're so upset and who has upset you."

Charles runs his fingers through his hair, holding it back he leans forward on his knees and asks, "You ever read Moby Dick?"

Mr. Deprimere sits forward with his elbows on his desk and says, “Of course.”

Charles says, “Ahab was a bad-ass.”

Mr. Deprimere laughs but Charles is serious. The moment is diffused for now, and both men have taken enough from the conversation. Mr. Deprimere asks, “When is your next show?”

“You’re going to come?”

Deprimere says, “I'll bring my wife.”

TWENTY-NINE

Pt. III

TWENTY-NINE

It would seem that spirits have no feeling, but spirits living or dead, past or present, existing are given depth, presence and purpose by their feelings. Ghosts of previous lives hold on because they can't let go. The living are no different, they too haunt the places that matter most.

Charles sits at the dinner table with his mother. She called him to invite him over and since Charles had no concrete plans he consented to a visit. That morning the maid had heard someone else in the house and when she got the courage up to go down stairs, no one was there. Looking out the front sitting room window she recognized Charles leaving the house. His mother took this news to mean Charles was calling out to her, that he had stayed the night was a cry for help. Never since high school had Charles and his mother stayed under the same roof and she was already worried about him. Mother had liked Isabel, not as a person but as a running mate for Charles. Then after the breakup she recognized the downward spiral in Charles much like she had seen in her husband twenty years earlier when they had their rows.

Claire serves a Dijon mustard glazed salmon encrusted with panko and herbs, "It's from such a remote part of Alaska that you can't buy it because they have no need for money, you have to trade with the locals. I have a chef friend that slipped me a box of fillets." She smiles at Charles and he likes the way her eyes shine, "It's served with a wild rice, but Charles, I better not see you mashing the two together. This salmon is on par with that bottle of Johnny Walker."

Mother smiles and says, "You understand?" and Charles says, "Yeah, you can't put that on ice."

Charles takes a bite and shuts his eyes, letting the flakes of fish come apart on his tongue, he chews the pinko grinding it slightly between his teeth, he eats a bit of rice and then washes it down with his scotch, after a moment he says to his mother, "I'm glad you invited me over."

His mother has a bite and dabs at her lips, she drinks her scotch and acts as if she is finished with dinner,

"If you need a place to stay we can take the desk out from the study and get a bed for you."

"I'm okay, mom."

"You look better."

Charles holds up a spoon and examines his distorted reflection, "I look terrible."

"You're right. But you look different. Whatever is different looks better."

Charles scoops up a spoon full of rice and then shoves a bit of salmon onto the end of the spoon, "Thanks, I guess," he says and then shovels the bite into his mouth.

A little while later Claire brings finger bowls filled with a small amount of hot water a wedge of lemon and long grain rice, she sets the first in front of Charles, the second goes to his mother. With his mother's back to Claire, Claire tilts her head indicating to Charles that he should follow.

"How was work?" his mother asks.

"I didn't go to work today."

"Did you let them know you weren't coming in?"

Charles dunks the tips of his fingers into the small bowl, “I've showed up in such a state over the years, they'll forgive me for missing a couple days.”

“Do you have some place to stay tonight?”

He looks through the doorway to the next room and he watches Claire straightening up in the kitchen.

“Do you have someplace to stay?” and for a while no one speaks, all three of them alive and healthy and alone in that house surrounded by spirits, none of them seeking to clear their name of the judgments made by the other.

*

TWENTY-NINE

Charles sits in front of his people and they shout at him. He acts like he doesn't care, but it is one of only a few things he really cares about. He smiles and they shout louder, he reads and they go silent, when he finishes a poem he drinks a shot and they shout at him, he puts the glass of beer to his lips and fills his mouth until he can take no more, he swallows wide and pours more beer into his mouth and they cheer.

Charles is supposed to be off stage by now, but he refuses and the crowd encourages him to keep reading. When Tommy shouts from behind the bar to Charles "Your time is up, come on down, Chuck. No more!" Tommy threatens to cut Chuck off and a girl in her early twenties hops up on stage. The girl gives her beer to Charles and she puts her arms around his neck, she kisses him on the lips, he doesn't kiss her back, he smiles modestly and lets her sit on his lap.

"You pick one, dear-heart." And the girl flips through his notebook. She looks over the poems while the crowd shouts. She blushes and Charles laughs, even Tommy laughs from behind the bar. Charles drinks the girl's beer.

She points to a poem and whispers in his ear.

"The girl has requested *There Have Been Times*," and the audience shouts back at him.

In the backroom of the bar Charles was seated behind a large oak desk, across from him a line of women trailed out the door, down the hallway and into the bar. A blonde woman in her early thirties leaned over the desk, her cleavage intentionally there to grab focus.

Charles asked, "Who should I make this out to?"

"Anna, Anna Lee," she waited another second before she spoke again, "BTW," and it made Charles cringed. Anna ended with, "I'm in love with not just your writing; I'm in love with you."

Charles handed her his book and says, "You've got terrible taste in men."

Her jeans are down around her ankles. Charles is leaned against the doorway that separates the kitchen from the living room of Anna Lee's apartment. Anna Lee grinds her ass into Charles crotch as he tries to balance himself.

Charles put on his aviators and drank a shot of whiskey while Sara handed him a copy, she said with a crooked smile,

"My boyfriend would be so pissed if he knew I was here. He hates that I read your stuff."

Charles drank his beer and looked up at her mocha skinned tight body.

"He's a writer too."

Charles arched his eyebrows from behind his sunglasses; it was a cliché but nevertheless true that he had little interest in other writers.

"He's good but he doesn't get me, he doesn't get that a little bit of grit under your nails can be a turn on."

Charles held up an open palm fist to inspect his fingernails, “Who should I make this out to?”

She smiled slowly, crooked and insinuating.

Charles stands next to a waterbed and Sara is lying on it wearing nothing except for her shoes. He sucks on the tips of her fingers while she has him inside her mouth.

He was sitting in a revolving chair behind the big oak desk and another woman slipped him her number. He looked at her wondering what her skin might feel like, he imagined what her apartment might be like, and he wondered with whom she first made love and what he was doing at that moment.

Charles liked being in the back office, he knew he didn’t belong there because he didn’t work at the bar, but he was the establishments biggest draw and they let him use the backroom to sign autographs because people waiting in line would then order drinks and mingle with the second wave of patrons, the locals, the regulars, the type that didn't give a shit about writing.

He was careful. Even though very little mattered, there was a lot at stake, it was important that Charles be cool, be kind and imply he would make love to his female readers without making it so candid that the experience would be shallow. No amount of admiration or respect turned people on to a meaningless fuck. Sex was an opportunity to believe, fully, and to be perceived as passionate.

Bridgette put one hand on the desk and leaned on it; she pulled her collar low and slid her first and middle finger down her breast grazing both sides of her nipple. She laughed to make the moment less intense in case Charles was put off, but Charles was very seldom put off.

In the kitchen of her apartment he turns Bridgette's back to him, putting his mouth on her ear Charles runs his hands over her body. She hums gently as he undoes the top of her jeans.

He stitches her neck with small kisses while she pulls off her underwear. Charles puts her hands against the refrigerator, he kneels underneath her and kisses between her thighs; she turns off the lights so that the neighbors can't see through the windows. She sticks a thumb in his mouth pinches her fingers under his chin and brings him to a standing position, she undoes his jeans, he steps out of them and grabs her around the waist, lifting her up she throws her legs around him and he slides inside her. They stay there standing with nothing to lean against, feeling every inch of each other, gravity brings them together and the weight of things doubles the intensity. They stay like that for a long time.

Cora was the last in line, once all the other girls cleared out, Cora handed Charles her copy of his first anthology and he made to sign it. She turned back to the door, threw it shut, turned the deadbolt and then charged toward him. She jumped on the desk, threw her legs over Charles shoulders and aimed her lovely ivory thighs at him.

*

TWENTY-NINE

Charles is surrounded by crude, pervasive graffiti. The room spins and he uses the sink to steady himself,

"Hi, Brett, hey... It's been a hot minute. Yeah, I just thought I should call you. 'Cause you know we had such a connection that one night. You know? I mean I was kinda laid back and you were coming on strong and I thought you know, maybe there was a miscommunication now that we're not talking, you know – this is a funny story, I thought you'd like this, a fan of mine said I should write a book. And I said fuck that. A book, right? Anyways, I'm kinda fucked up. Books aren't really interesting unless the protagonist is like a figure head for a culture, or not culture, what is the word I'm looking for... fucking writers should be good with words. Anyways, I was thinking about you and how maybe there was some miscommunication and I upset you or hurt your feelings, and I just wanted to put that out there, I didn't want to be like everyone else our age, like they're an entire generation of text messaging socially inept youth propped up on flaccid back bones--Anyways."

Charles looks at his phone to see how long he's been on it.

"Era. That's the word I was looking for. Era."

He tries to focus on his reflection in the mirror, "F--uck, this is a long--"

*

Charles and Claire eat leftovers from a large glass salad bowl. It's the middle of the night and neither is speaking. They eat bits of corkscrew pasta off the tips of long thin forks made of silver. The sundried tomatoes are overpowering but the flavor from the earthy portabella mixed with the oil neutralizes the acidic element.

Charles chews slowly.

"When was the last time you ate?"

Charles doesn't answer.

"I heard you quit your job."

Charles doesn't respond.

"You quit your job, the job that paid you to write about alcohol? You got paid to review beer and liquor? And you just quit?"

Charles swallows dryly and says, "I fail to understand your infusions."

Claire washes down her last bite with a mouthful of wine.

"*Inflections*."

"It was a blog."

"Blogs *are* writing. You're not an eighty-year-old man. If you want to write you'll have to write where people read. Every artist takes a day job."

Charles stabs clumps of spinach and mushroom with his fork and compliments her cooking, "This is—really—fucking good."

"I know."

Thinking of nothing to say, without thinking Charles says, "Do you want to-- do you have... have… a boyfriend?"

She blinks twice, surprised, she blinks twice more, "Chuck, I'm married. I have two kids at home."

She looks at him closely.

"My husband and I aren't on the best of terms but we are *together*."

"What is going on?"

"With what?"

"With us?"

"Us? Charles you don't know the first thing about me."

"No-- but... kids?"

"Yes."

Charles opens another bottle of wine and asks, "How old are they?"

"My boy is five years old and my baby girl is two."

"Are they amazing?"

"You know how good that pasta tastes?"

"Incredible."

"That's love. I put myself and my love into everything I do."

They are both quiet for a minute and then Charles mumbles, "Homiletic." Claire laughs first, then Charles joins her, the laughter runs its course, they catch their breath and then it is quiet again.

*

The server is small, too small for Charles, her arms are as thin as his wrists, but he likes her, her skin is tight against her small frame, her eyes set back, her lips of a European decent, she's pretty enough to be a model but she doesn't know it. Charles is taken with her, and he wants her to like him. She laughs and he smiles.

He sits in front of a beer and a shot and when he pauses mid-story about a crazy ex-girlfriend that made him set a beloved T-shirt on fire because another girl, years earlier had given it to him as gift, Charles drinks just the shot of whiskey. The server might want to get away to attend her tables but she is polite enough not to let on, she humors Charles, which is bad because the longer he talks the more enamored he becomes with the girl.

When she looks over at her tables Charles takes in her physic, though she sports a dangerously low body fat she has breasts, not large but lovely, she has olive skin though she's blonde and Charles keeps going on, talking her ear off, "Like a favorite sweater you can't let go, it's something you never want to throw out."

"I've had the same favorite pair of shoes for five years."

"That's nothing, rookie. I've had my favorite T-shirt for fifteen years. I don't wear it out of the house. I keep it someplace safe, hidden away, just for me," Charles sips his beer, "That's what women are."

The server arches her eyebrows and asks him, "Objects?"

Floundering, Charles' hands come to life moving in exaggerated ways to explain what he is saying, "No, not women, relationships. No matter how long you hold onto them they get tattered."

"Or closer to your heart," she beams optimistic.

"No. I'm mixing-- I'm saying, at some point you have to say this thing has outlived its purpose."

"Seriously?"

"You can't wear a shirt that's got stains, not in public. And a self-respecting person wouldn't even keep stained clothes to wear around the house, no matter how comfortable or sentimental."

"How about you just tell me what you're trying to say."

"I'd like to run my fingers through your hair till I know we won't work. And I'll kiss you gently and say something sweet as we go our separate ways."

The moment would be uncomfortable except that they are both still smiling, "How do you know I'd go for it?"

Charles eyes her carefully, "Hmm, I sense resistance?"

"I didn't say that."

Charles drinks the rest of his beer, "People are always trying to *make things work* and I'm the asshole because I have the foresight to say that: nothing ever does."

The server takes Charles' empty glasses and sets them behind the bar. She smiles at him and goes in the back, thinking from other instances this is a nonverbal invitation to follow her, Charles gets off his barstool and heads in the direction that she disappeared. From seemingly nowhere Tommy's ropey forearm shoves Charles back against the bar.

"Fuck!"

“What the fuck do you think, Chuck?”

“Don't put your fuckin' hands on me.”

“I'll fucking break your hands if you say another word to my niece.”

“What are you talking about, she's a cute girl, so you talk to me like I'm a rapist?”

“In a word?”

“Fuck. Fuck you, dick.”

“You want to spend the night in jail?”

“Seriously?”

Tommy the bartender, the retired professional wrestler leans into Charles ear and whispers.

Charles composes himself, “Okay. Wow. I'm done.”

“Get out.”

“Stop.”

TWENTY-NINE

"Get out now!"

Steadying himself Charles shoves off from the bar and adjusts the collar of his shirt. He peels a twenty from his billfold and tosses it over his shoulder.

In his car Charles sits with his sunglasses on, smoking cigarettes and watching people walking past going somewhere, people waiting for the bus, late for work, buying lottery tickets, people jogging; Charles does a bump.

Inside Mr. Deprimere's office Charles wanders the carpet. He walks from one end to the other looking at patterns. There is a sitting chair near the window and he sits on the arm. Outside the world is bright and the clouds look like waves on the surface of an angry ocean.

Charles wonders how long Mr. Deprimere has been working out of this office. How many people he has counseled, how many people has he helped? Charles sits at Mr. Deprimere's desk and wonders if he could have been a therapist, could he have been a psychiatrist, could he have even been a guidance counselor? Bored and unsure why he is in this office alone Charles does another bump.

He looks up at a wall clock hanging next to the door to the office. It is strategically placed so that during sessions Mr.

Deprimere can see the clock and check the time without his patient knowing, because checking his watch could be insulting. Mr. Deprimere is late. Charles has never been early for one of their appointments so he cannot be sure if it is unusual.

Fixing to do something, anything, he picks up Mr. Deprimere's phone and Charles dials a number, "Hey this is Charles, leave us a--" Charles inputs a four digit number to listen to his voicemail messages.

The automated voice tells him he has five new messages. The first message begins and at first Charles doesn't recognize the voice,

"So, um… you're gone."

Charles presses seven, message deleted. Next message,

"Hey it's Liza again, call me when you get this."

Charles presses seven deleting the message. The next message starts,

"Go FUCK yourself, Charles--"

Charles deletes the message.

A man's voice says 'It's me,' the message is from his father. Charles deletes the message. Next new message,

"Chuck, Charlie whatever the fuck you want to be called..." It's Mr. Deprimere's voice, "I'm not sure why I'm even bothering to call. I don't have to tell you that you missed your court date because I've told you half a dozen times for the last month that it was this morning. What I do have to tell you is that it's going to be a long time before the state of California lets you drive again, which probably means nothing to you, but when they do get you for driving around like you have a license--"

Charles drops the phone on the desk and puts his head in his hands; and the thing of it is, the thing that really upsets him is that Charles honestly believed today was going to be a good day.

*

That day he went outside to walk his father's dog. Up until that moment of all the things that he gave notice, it was the most important that he pushed away. It was an uncharacteristic day, ugly and humid, already dark in the afternoon. A random day like any other, with no attachments, no recollection of the events leading up to this moment, just a random unattached memory, but he was conscious enough to wonder how the hell he ended up there. Last night where had he fallen asleep, where had he woken up? Was there a girl there? And if there was, was it one of his girls or someone new to 'the let down?' If she was a new girl would she have thick skin and breathe easy knowing that night between the sheets spent with Charles was sex without love, like fast-food that wouldn't clog up the inside, liquor without liver damage, fun without merit. Charles was vacant. He wasn't a catch; he was a rebound, a fantasy, a dream keeper to make women feel pretty. Anything of substance with the opposite sex was over before it happened and to go longer than an evening meant pratfalls, lies and misdirection. It wasn't an issue of pride, unless they made it about pride, pride led to vendettas and justice was a hinged shank of a rusted anchor in the hearts of men and women. Had he ever done the wrong thing? In a hundred thousand times when he was alone with a woman had he ever been inappropriate? He had only done what their body told him, he had never meant to hurt anyone's feelings, he had no malicious intent. No intent to harm moved his hands. He felt hung-over but he was very, very drunk, at no other point in his life had he ever felt so old. His ankles hurt from days spent walking barefoot; he kept a pair of shoes in the car when he needed to go into liquor stores or bars that he was unfamiliar with, but more often he walked barefoot. That morning the gravel of the road in their gated community was too rough to walk without some kind of footwear so he put on thong sandals. The flip-flop sound trailed behind him and Pax. And at times he thought about his father and how distant his father was and whether that made Charles distant from his father and from women and from everyone else. But it wasn't his intention to blame his father for the man he had become. Every time he seemed to have a notion of what, why and when, whenever he seemed to be able to put a pin in that ever elusive cause, that ghost that was to blame, whoever it belonged to it would suddenly and without warning disappear. He did his best to keep a straight line as he walked Pax, he felt disabled, unable to connect with any of the people in his life, the people he had once loved always fell away becoming extinct in a fog of misunderstanding and miscommunications. And though he was free, he was sad. Tears meant nothing, as he couldn't cry, *boys don't cry* but more accurate is that: men *can't* cry. Simultaneously a man could ask *what have I done* while being pounded with the reality of how unfair and cruel and misleading the things that he had done could be deemed.

And did it matter what it was?

Every woman was an opportunity to feel humility, nervousness, rejection, acceptance, confidence and validity. At that moment Charles stepped awkwardly and the plastic strap on his flip-flop ripped apart. He stumbled and letting go the leash he fell flat, hitting the asphalt his crumpled unlit cigarette bounced from the impact and flew from his lips. The front of Charles shoulder absorbed most of the collision, except a bit of the jaw on his right profile got thrashed. A minute later he used his arms to push himself up, got a leg under him and then shoved himself to a standing position.

Brushing loose bits of gravel stuck into his palms Charles balances on two feet and assesses the situation thinking, okay, not so bad. Until he realizes that he had let go the leash and Pax was gone. Charles looks in all directions and Pax is nowhere in sight, he whips his head in one direction and the other and nearly loses balance.

Charles sees the hole in the chain link fence.

Charles rushes barefoot toward the fence, without slowing, he puts his hands on the fence and then throws his legs over the side vaulting onto the other side, onto the freeway he runs into traffic. He looks in all directions, he stands in the middle of the freeway, hit with a sudden desperation he gives up and so overwhelmed by the moment he sits down in the median that separates north and south bound traffic.

Charles comes through the front door and he looks at his father. A weird unexamined silence fills the house. Both of them knowing something should be said. Charles is winded; when his father looks at his son he can tell something is wrong.

TWENTY-NINE

Getting to his feet the old warrior asks, "What's the matter?"

Finally getting his breath Charles undoes the clasp on Pax's leash letting her loose in the house. Charles says, "Nothing."

"Charles, you have a reading tonight, don't you?"

"Do you want to come?"

"No, you know I don't like to be around those people. I was going to say if you needed a ride I would drop you off."

Charles looks at his father and really sees him; Charles sees who he is and where he's come from. He looks at his father as a man, a good man; but also as a destination.

"Do well tonight, son." Here his father puts his hands on his son and says, "You could try to... class it up a little."

Charles' father pulls up to the curb, they shake hands and then Charles gets out of the car. Some people standing outside smoking cigarettes spot Charles, they shout at him and raise their fists in the air. Charles does the same and then one of the girls hugs him around the chest and kisses him on the ear, her boyfriend pulls her off Charles and most of them laugh about it. Charles gets to the door, he pulls it open and it swings wide. The music is blasting, it pounds in Charles ears and he goes inside.

People don't really see him, everyone is focused on each other's lips, people have to shout to be heard. People have their heads turned to better hear each other. There are others that have their heads down sending text messages waiting for the show to start. No one's point is fully understood, but it's fine because that evening no one has a meaningful point.

Charles spots Tommy the bartender and makes his way over to him. They exchange a few words and nod to one another, Tommy can't hear Charles but he knows what he is saying, and so he nods. A second later they shake hands and Tommy pulls Charles into his chest, their arms go around each other and their hands clap each other on the back.

Charles squeezes past a group of people and when he loses balance they hold Charles up and he tells them it is okay, he's not drunk he's just a bit nervous and his readers cackle with eager laughs at such a preposterous concept. This triggers a reaction in him as he is often nervous, because, especially when he is sober he is almost consistently nervous. He charms his way left to get out of this weird moment of personal realization and just then he sees Claire from across the room. He steps toward her but at a second glance he realizes it isn't Claire, though the woman resembles her in a distant way, physically, she looks nothing like her. As a girl comes toward him suddenly, as he catches her eye he recognizes Liza, she puts her arms around his neck, Charles is surprised by such a warm welcome, when she pulls away she's someone else, someone not Liza, a woman Charles has never met. She screams over the music "I love your writing," and Charles kisses her forehead and gently moves her aside. A hand on his arm pulls him against the bar. He follows the hand up to the shoulder and sees Amy's big brown eyes. She says something he can't hear. Charles turns his ear to her and she says it again, "I want you to meet my boyfriend." Charles puts out his hand to shake and the man next to her takes it. The man smiles at Charles, and he must be a fan because if any man is introduced by a woman to Charles, a man has to suspect their past, because women have a way of telling the truth with their eyes even if their mouth says 'he's an old friend.' Amy points to the other side of the bar and shouts something Charles can't hear, but when he looks in that direction he sees a familiar girl standing there and instantly recognizes her. Charles says goodbye to Amy and her boyfriend and then he walks the long anxious journey to say hello, intermittently he stops to thank a friend, or sign a book, eventually he makes it to the other side of the bar and he stops in front of the blonde and they force themselves to make eye contact, a starring game where no one wins but the loser forfeits everything. Despite the apprehension on her face they talk long enough that a civility is established and they even hug. She says, "Happy Birthday, Charles" and he says "Thank you, Isabel."

Charles gets up on stage and takes the microphone. He looks out at the audience and groans, "Would you look at all these ugly people." They roar with applause. Tommy's niece comes up on stage and sets a beer and a shot on the stool next to Charles; he aims the microphone away and whispers in the girl's ear. She nods and smiles and says with clever eyes, "We're cool," and Charles swells with redoubled confidence. The girl squeezes his forearm and walks off stage. Charles looks out over the crowd and with the stage lights in his eyes, the sound of the crowd demanding that he begin, the smell of the bar reeks from spilled beer, perfume and pheromones, the microphone feels like a gun, cold and heavy.

Charles smiles with shinning eyes and shouts to the crowd,

"FUCK POETRY!... I want to buy you a drink."

TWENTY-NINE

www.AaronDoolittle.com

www.ingramcontent.com/pod-product-compliance
Ingram Content Group UK Ltd.
Pitfield, Milton Keynes, MK11 3LW, UK
UKHW041942190726
13854UKWH00004B/1741

9 781105 354595